Sinful Desires

An Enemies to Lovers Erotic Romance
by
Reba Bale

Table of Contents

---

1. https://paperorpixels.com/

About This Book

She pretends to be pious, but she's about to be corrupted.

Hank:

Maribel Andrews, aka "The Church Lady", has fascinated me for as long as I can remember. I've always wondered if those prim outfits and severe hairstyles hid a secret. Little did I know that Maribel had a kinky side, one I longed to dominate...

Maribel:

For years I was the "good girl", doing what was expected of me. I saved myself for marriage, turned a blind eye to my husband's cheating, and faithfully went to church every week to pray for my salvation. Until the day I realized my salvation wasn't up in the heavens, it was right there with the bad boy working at our small-town grocery store.

Soon I'm engaging in increasingly creative and sensual activities, exploring my submissive side, and pushing my sexual boundaries until the one thing I never expected happened...I fell in love.

"Sinful Desires" is a steamy, light BDSM, humorous erotic romance, with a midlife couple who have an unexpectedly happy ending.

Be sure to check out a free preview of "Summer in Paradise: A MFM Romance" at the end of this book!

Dedication

For every person who tried their best to be the good girl, then fell for the bad boy. You're never too old to get corrupted. Or have some fun.

Join My Newsletter

Want a free book? Join my newsletter and receive a copy of my book "Hotwife Happy Hour" for free. I promise I will only email you when there are new releases or special sales, usually twice a month. Visit my newsletter sign-up page[1] at bit.ly/rebabooks to join today.

Hank

Every week I'd see her come into my grocery store after church. Maribel Andrews. She was the kind of uptight that you only got in a small town. Churchy. Judgmental. Gossipy. And more in need of a good fucking than any woman I knew.

She was a good-looking woman, although she did her best to hide it behind her prim outfits and severe hairstyle. But even that pinched look of disapproval that she wore like a mask wasn't enough to hide the beauty of those high cheekbones, wide brown eyes, and that creamy white skin that I longed to mark.

Maribel had been in the periphery of my life for quite a while now. I'd guess she was about thirty-eight or so, maybe forty. She'd married her high school sweetheart and never left this small town where she was born and raised.

Everyone knew about the cheating except for her. It was no small irony that while she was judging everyone she believed lived a life of sin her husband — ex-husband now — was tomcatting around with any woman who'd spread their legs for him. And that was a surprisingly large number, given old Ted's reputation as a stud in the sack.

Maribel had been the star of some of my dirtiest fantasies as long as I could remember. I was a fair bit younger than her, having just turned thirty, and the only time in the last ten years I'd stepped foot in church was my daddy's funeral, so we didn't exactly run in the same circles. But I'd watched her, nonetheless.

Something about her fascinated me. And I suspected that the feeling was mutual because barely a week went by that I didn't catch her studying me while I was at work or watching me ride down the street on my motorcycle, a look of unguarded lust on her face if she thought no one was paying her any attention. She didn't want to be attracted to me but damned if she wasn't.

Since my daddy died I'd taken over as the general manager of our family grocery store, a store that had been a mainstay in our town for nearly a hundred years. Since many of my employees were church-going folks, I was always glad to take the Sunday morning shift. Especially since it gave me an opportunity to watch Maribel.

I rarely talked to her, but I always watched her.

She usually came in around eleven-thirty, feeling freshly pious after the ten o'clock church service she attended. Today she was wearing a pale blue suit with tiny white checks. It looked thick, like maybe it was wool or something, the skirt coming precisely three inches below her knees. Any higher would be unseemly, no doubt. The jacket covered most of her pristine white blouse, a little bow tied at the collar. The only thing uglier than her outfit was her plain black pumps with a square two-inch heel.

Maribel had her blonde hair pulled back in a bun so tight it was a wonder she got any circulation to her face. She didn't wear a speck of make-up as far as I could tell, not that she needed it. Her beauty was natural. Unfortunately, it appeared to be only skin deep.

I'd developed an elaborate fantasy about her, one that involved spanking and face fucking and all sorts of corruption. But I'd never thought that I'd be able to make that a reality. Until today.

"Excuse me, sir."

Her voice was cold as ice.

"It's Hank, Maribel, you know that. Just like my daddy."

I didn't try to hide my irritation. A tiny twitch in her eye was the only sign she'd heard me.

"I'm looking for a pork loin, but I don't see any in the meat cooler."

"Let me have a look."

I let her walk ahead of me, mostly so I could stare at the flex of those round globes of her ass. Even that hideous skirt couldn't fully hide her shapely curves. For the thousandth time I wondered what she looked like underneath those unflattering clothes.

When we got to the meat department I looked at the display case to verify that we didn't have the cut of meat she wanted. I knew we'd gotten a shipment of pork today.

"I think we have some more pork back in the meat locker," I told her. "Lemme check."

"I want the pork loin," she said, emphasizing the word "loin" in a way that made my dick twitch.

"Got it."

"I don't want one with too much fat, I want a lean cut of meat."

"Okay."

"It needs to be fresh." She said that as if we had a reputation for bad meat.

"That's all we sell."

"I want one that's at least two pounds but no more than five."

I could feel my frustration growing as she followed me towards the back door, yammering at me the whole way in that bossy voice.

"Maybe you just want to come in the meat locker and pick it out yourself," I said smartly.

"Maybe I do."

"Fine."

I led her through the dry storage room, noting that the space was empty right now, and pulled open the heavy door leading to the meat locker. It was basically a large, refrigerated room, well-organized with rows of meat neatly stacked and labeled. The space was lit by a single lightbulb, leaving the corners in shadow.

I reached up on a shelf to pull down a box of meat and when I turned, Maribel was staring at my ass, practically salivating.

"Like what you see?" I asked.

Even in the dim light, I could see her face flush.

"I was merely watching to make sure you didn't pull a muscle or something."

"I got a muscle you can pull."

"What?" she looked confused at my bad innuendo.

"You know what your problem is Miz Maribel?"

I took a step closer, forcing her to look up at me. I had a good six inches on her, even with the added height of her sensible pumps.

"What, pray tell, is my problem?" Her eyes snapped.

"You need to get fucked. And good."

Her mouth opened in a gasp of outrage. "How dare you?"

"How dare *you* walk around town acting so high and mighty like you're better than the rest of us peons?"

Our eyes locked in a long glare and to my everlasting shock, Maribel Andrews flew towards me so fast that I backed into the shelf behind me. One small hand fisted in my hair, pulling my head down, and our mouths met in an angry mash of teeth and lips.

God damn that felt good. I let her kiss me for a hot minute, then pulled back to meet her gaze again.

"Your actions seem to imply that you're gonna take my advice and let me fuck the mean out of you."

Another outraged gasp.

"You are not a polite person," she said, as if that was the worse insult she could throw at me.

"I never claimed to be nice or polite. But I got something you need, Miz Maribel."

To illustrate my point, I reached down and palmed my erection. Her eyes followed my hand and damn near popped out of her head like a cartoon character. But she didn't run away screaming like I might have expected.

When she just stood there gaping at me with her mouth open like a damn fish, I added, "I need you to say it, so there's no misunderstanding about what we're doing here."

I pulled her close to me, pressing my erection against her belly, and grabbing two fistfuls of that incredible ass. "Tell me what you want."

She hesitated for so long I thought for sure she was going to hightail it out of there despite that look of obvious desire on her face. Maybe it was just my imagination, but I swear I could smell her arousal in the confined space of the cooler.

"Please." Her voice was little more than a whisper.

"Please what?"

"It's been a long time. I have...needs."

I figured that was the best articulation of consent I was going to get. I lowered my mouth to hers, giving her a crushing kiss that left us both breathless. When I pulled away, her lips were red and swollen, and I found that I quite liked that look on her.

Without another word I reached behind her and unzipped her skirt. She helped me shimmy it off her legs and then I unzipped my jeans while she worked on removing her plain white panties. I lowered my pants just enough to free my dick, and I damn near came on the spot when I saw her stare at my erection and lick her lips. Clearly Mis Maribel liked what I was packing.

With a growl I spun her around to face the row of shelves, reaching for her hands and placing them on the edge. A hand between her shoulder blades got her into a position that I liked, bent over, ass out. I tapped my shoe between her feet, and she heeded my unspoken command to spread her legs.

My eyes took in the milky white globes of her ass and the sheen of moisture on her pussy. She was natural of course. Nothing so lowbrow as waxing for our resident Church Lady. But that area appeared neatly groomed, so I had no complaints. I liked my women to look like women, not little girls.

I lowered myself over her back and kissed along the side of her neck before nipping her ear.

"You gotta be quiet," I said. "You look like you might be a screamer."

Really, the sound didn't travel too much through the thick walls of the meat locker, but I wanted to ramp up the anticipation.

I took my dick in hand and slid it up and down her folds a few times, getting it nice and lubricated. Maribel let out a soft moan. Then, when she was least expecting it, I laid my palm across her ass in a stinging slap.

Thwack!

"Hey!"

I slapped her other cheek. "Be quiet now, you want the whole town to hear you?"

By the fourth smack she'd stopped protesting, and right around the sixth, she started pushing back to meet my hand. Somehow I'd always known that my little Church Lady was kinky. I was betting her husband never wrecked her the way she needed to be wrecked. No, despite his reputation with the ladies, I was betting old Ted was strictly a missionary man. At least with his wife.

After getting her ass nice and red I was ready to commence with the fucking. I gripped her cheeks, one in each hand, and spread her wide enough to watch myself slide into that tight little pussy. We both moaned as I fed myself into her, much slower than I would have preferred, but she was too damned tight to do much else. When I finally bottomed out deep inside her, I considered it a victory.

Moving my hands to grip the curve of her hips, I started pounding into Maribel so hard it was a miracle I didn't send her flying right up onto the shelf between the boxes of meat. Her fingers were white as they gripped the shelves, giving her leverage to push back against me. I made absolutely no effort to be gentle because that was the last thing she needed. Somehow I knew that instinctively.

I released her hip and moved my hand up to grip that tightly wound bun, pulling her head back and keeping her totally under my control.

"Oh my God!"

"Your God's not much use to you in here, not while I'm fucking your sweet pussy."

"You're disgusting."

"You're a shrew."

"You're a bad man."

That was the last insult she hurled before she went off like a rocket. She made the most ungodly shrieking noise as her body bucked beneath mine. I knew she would be a screamer.

Her inner muscles contracted around me until I followed her over the edge, groaning as I spurted my cum deep inside her.

She was still shaking when I pulled out, using the hem of my shirt to wipe our juices off my dick, and tucked myself back into my pants.

Maribel stayed in position for a full minute, chest heaving, ass quivering as she recovered from her own release. I couldn't help but admire the twin spots of red that I'd left on her pale white skin.

I heard her take a deep breath before she stood back up then slowly pulled that ugly conservative skirt down over her hips, covering herself. She avoided my gaze as she found her virginal panties on the floor, pulling them over her feet and shimmying them back up her hips. Only when she was fully dressed again did she meet my gaze.

"I guess you were right, I needed that."

And without another word Miz Maribel marched out of my meat locker, her spine ramrod straight as she headed out to finish her weekly grocery shopping.

Maribel

"Darn it!"

I stared in dismay at my tire. I'd been driving home from work when my car suddenly made a loud noise that sounded like a gunshot, immediately followed by my car violently pulling to the right. Fortunately, no one was driving near me, and I was able to safely pull over to park on the shoulder.

Sure enough, my tire was completely flat. I had no idea how to fix it, so I pulled out my phone to call for help. I winced when I realized I was in a dead zone and had no cell service.

"Darn it!"

I was almost tempted to say a real swear word, but my mama had taught me to be a lady. Fat lot of good it did. I'd done everything "right", just the way she taught me. Dressed conservatively. Saved myself for marriage. Put up with a husband who slept with every slut who spread her legs. Went to church every week without fail. I'd never done anything but be one hundred percent proper.

At least until last week...

My face heated as I remembered my shameful behavior last Sunday. I'd stopped in Parson's grocery store right after church, the same way I did every week. I was nothing if not a creature of habit. I'd wanted to get a pork loin, but they didn't have any, so I'd fetched Hank, the owner, to find one for me.

Hank. Goodness, he was a fine specimen. He was about eight years younger than me, scarcely thirty, with thick dark hair, broad shoulders, a muscled torso, and legs like tree trunks. The man didn't have an ounce of fat on him.

I'd be lying if I said he didn't fascinate me, but I never would have acted on that. Proper women like me didn't hang around with men like that. He didn't go to church. And worse yet, he drove a motorcycle. He was what my mama would have called "a bad boy".

Despite our differences, we'd found ourselves having a little interlude in the grocery store meat locker. I laughed at myself. *Interlude Maribel? How about dirty, rough, and incredibly hot sex?*

At thirty-eight years old I'd had my first sexual experience outside of marriage. My first spanking. And may the good Lord help me, my first orgasm. I finally understood what all the fuss was about. My nether regions were still tingling from that orgasm.

I'd been a little off kilter ever since then. It had been wrong, but gosh it had felt right. Nevertheless, I hadn't stepped foot in the grocery store since it happened.

I heard the roar of a motorcycle coming down the hill. I stepped out into the road to wave the person down. This stretch of road was usually pretty deserted at this time of the day. Chances were good that whoever was coming by was someone I knew, and I didn't want to miss a chance to get help.

As the motorcycle got closer, my heart started to pound. The rider's shape looked familiar. He pulled to the side of the road behind my car, pulling off his helmet, and sure enough, it was Hank Parsons. The man I'd let defile me in the meat locker.

He was wearing faded jeans that looked like they were painted on his thick thighs, along with a tight white tee shirt, a black leather jacket, and black boots. He looked like everyone's bad boy fantasy come to life.

"Hey there."

I gave him an awkward wave. What was the protocol for when you ran into someone after doing what we'd done? Darned if I knew.

"Well Maribel Andrews," he drawled. "What kind of trouble have you gotten yourself into here?"

My spine snapped straight, and I gave him the haughty look I'd learned from my mother. God rest her soul, but Jesus Christ himself would probably find a way to disappoint that woman.

"I blew out my tire."

He glanced from me to the car, one corner of his mouth lifting into that crooked smirk that always made my heart flutter.

"Let me guess. You don't know how to change a tire." His tone made it clear that he found me lacking.

"My husband always took care of things like that."

He rolled his eyes. "I hear tell you don't have a husband anymore, Miz Maribel."

I nodded. He'd heard right. After Ted managed to impregnate the preacher's twenty-two-year-old niece, they'd both practically been run out of town on a rail. I'd filed for divorce the day after I found out. I'd been raised to believe that marriage was a lifetime commitment, and I'd put up with a lot from that man over the years. But knocking up some little tart was the last straw. Even my poor dead mama would have backed me up on that one.

"Can you help me?" I asked. "Please?"

He sauntered over to the car. Hank never walked anywhere. He strode, he sauntered, or he stalked. It was incredibly attractive.

"Pop the trunk."

I pressed the button on the key fob and the trunk popped open with a click. He leaned into the opening, rooting around for the spare tire and the jack, and my eyes fixed firmly on his muscled rear end, lovingly molded by his ancient blue jeans. I hadn't gotten a good look at it during our little interlude — probably because Hank had leaned me over a shelf and pounded into me from behind — but I'd watched him enough to know that he had the best ass in our small town. No doubt about it.

After finding the jack and the spare tire he got to work while I stood there feeling useless. He made quick work of loosening the lug nuts, jacking up the car, and switching out the tire. As he lowered the car back to the ground, he called over his shoulder, "You shouldn't drive too fast on this donut. Try to keep it under thirty-five if you can. And no unnecessary trips. You go right to the auto shop in the morning and get this replaced."

"Okay."

I shouldn't like him bossing me around. I'd hated it when my husband did that. But for some reason, I didn't mind it so much with Hank.

"That does it." He slammed the trunk closed.

"Hold on a minute please."

I walked to the passenger side, reaching into my purse. After a moment's consideration, I pulled out three twenties. That should be a good payment for changing a tire, right? When I turned around, he was standing right behind me, watching me with narrowed eyes.

"What are you doing?"

I thrust the sixty dollars towards him. "I want to pay you for your troubles. Thank you very much for your help."

His eyes narrowed and a flush rose up his cheeks, visible even in the fading light of dusk.

"I don't want your damn money," he growled.

I realized that I'd offended him, but if there was one thing I didn't want, it was to owe someone something. I'd fought hard to become my own woman after the divorce, and there was no way I was going back.

"I want to pay you," I insisted stubbornly, thrusting the money towards him again.

He grabbed it out of my hand and tossed it over my shoulder onto the floor of my car. Then he stalked closer until I was trapped between him and the open car door. Maybe I should have been afraid, but instead, my panties grew damp with excitement. It was entirely a new phenomenon. I couldn't think of a single time when my ex-husband had dampened my panties.

"You want to pay me, Miz Maribel?"

He glanced meaningfully at his groin. My eyes widened as I saw the bulge there. Clearly our sparring excited him as much as it did me.

"How about you give me some relief?" he snapped. "I've been half hard for you ever since you walked out of that meat locker last Sunday.

I know you spend a lot of time on your knees Miz Maribel, maybe you could put all that kneeling to good use."

His eyes held a challenge, and I knew instinctively that he thought I'd back down. It showed how little he knew me. Without a word, I dropped to my knees right there on the side of the road. Hank's mouth dropped open in shock.

The gravel dug into my bare knees, but I welcomed the pain. I gave him a triumphant little smile as I reached up and unzipped his jeans. I slid them down to his knees, then reached for his boxers. They had motorcycles on them, which seemed fitting. Stretching the waistband over his erect penis, I pushed his boxers down as well.

My word, this man had a beautiful penis. *Cock Maribel,* the voice in my head chided me. *You can call it a cock.* That particular voice had been getting more and more forceful the longer I was divorced.

I leaned forward and pressed a tiny kiss against the tip of Hank's cock. It was long and thick, with the tiniest curve near the head.

I'd never thought of manly parts as attractive before, but then again the only one I'd ever seen was my husband's. I'd figured he was about average, but now I was wondering if that was correct, because Hank was significantly bigger. I couldn't even get my hand all the way around him, although I tried.

Gripping him as tightly as I could, I began sliding my hand back and forth a few times. There was a bit of friction, so I licked my hand to give it some moisture. Hank made the most unusual groaning noise.

I shuffled forward a few more inches and began to explore the mushroom head of his cock with my tongue while I jacked him off with my hand. I swirled my tongue around and under the tip a few times before opening wider and sliding down his length. He was so big I couldn't get it all in before he hit the back of my throat.

I slid back and forth, getting a good rhythm going, one hand gripping his butt cheek, the other his thigh.

Glancing up at Hank from beneath my lashes, I whispered, "You taste good."

"Take down your hair."

"What?"

"Get those pins out of your hair before I rip them out." His voice was as rough as the gravel I was kneeling on.

I picked out a few bobby pins that held my hair in place then pulled out the clip that held it into a bun. I breathed a sigh of relief as I always did when I let my hair down. It was my second favorite part of the day — second only to taking off my bra. My long blonde hair fell to my shoulders in a mess of waves.

"I knew it," he whispered.

One large hand slid through the strands and then gripped the back of my head, pulling me back towards his cock. With a deep growl, Hank took over, guiding my mouth up and down his member in a steady rhythm.

My jaw was open near as wide as it would go, and Hank was moving so roughly I gripped his thighs to keep my balance. Every time he hit the back of my throat I had to fight my gag reflex, but as I relaxed more, he was able to drive the tip right in.

"That's right Miz Maribel, you deep-throat me like a good girl."

I shivered in excitement at his illicit words. I'd given my husband a million blow jobs — after all that was expected as a wife I supposed — but this was the first time I'd actually liked it. The first time it made me feel powerful. The first time it had turned me on.

The roughness, the passion, the unique taste of his pre-cum dripping in my mouth, it was all different than anything I'd ever experienced. And the idea of being caught here on my knees on the side of the road, giving a blow job to a man I wasn't even married to, well that just ramped up my excitement. I could feel my lady parts dripping with arousal.

I curved my tongue a bit so I could slide it along the bottom of his shaft, then hollowed out my cheeks, giving him some good, hard suction. Hank groaned in approval.

"You like being face fucked on the side of the road Miz Maribel?" he grit out. "You like being on your knees like a little slut for me?"

God help me but I sure did. I couldn't help but nod. His motions became erratic, and I reached around to squeeze his balls gently. Then I hummed against his cock.

"Maribel!"

That was all the notice I got before he started releasing his cum into my mouth. I swallowed furiously, trying to drink it all down but it was too much. Cum mixed with my own saliva and dripped down my chin and then lower, dampening my blouse.

Hank pulled out slowly, looking a little dazed. I leaned forward, licking his dick clean, and his eyes glowed with approval.

"Do you know how many times I imagined fucking your mouth?" he asked as he pulled up his pants and zipped himself back to being decent. "How often I've dreamed of corrupting you?"

I shook my head.

"A shockingly high number of times."

He reached for my hand, pulling me up to standing. Our eyes met and held for a long moment. I thought he was going to kiss me, but instead, he gave me a curt nod.

"Your debt to me is paid. Don't forget to get that tire fixed."

I was still standing there gaping at him when he roared off down the road, leaving me a hot and horny mess.

Hank

There comes a time in every man's life when he comes face to face with his own mortality. I expected to be older when it happened, honestly, but here I was at age thirty feeling my heart pounding so loud in my chest that I was pretty sure I was having a heart attack.

Cause of death? One Maribel Andrews. Or as I liked to secretly call her, "The Church Lady".

"What are you doing here Miz Maribel?" I asked the woman who was currently standing on my porch wearing conservative black pumps and a long trench coat that was cinched at the waist.

She licked her lips nervously and my eyes followed the motion. I knew from experience that those lips were soft and full and looked incredible when they were wrapped around my cock.

"After our two, um, interludes, I was hoping you would allow me a few minutes to discuss what I believe is a mutually beneficial proposal."

She always talked in that snooty way, it was one of the things I both loved and hated about her. I'd always figured her for a cold fish, what with the way she'd walked around with her nose in the air for years. Maribel was one of those gossipy church people who seemed to sit in judgment over every person in town.

Or at least I thought she was. She'd been acting different since her cheating ex got run out of town. I'd always been weirdly fascinated with her, but after she let me fuck her in a meat locker, I started to wonder if there was more to Miz Maribel than met the eye. When she dropped to her knees and gave me the best blowjob of my life on the side of the road a few days ago, I became aware of two things: there was more to Maribel than met the eye, and I liked her a bit more than I should.

"What's your proposal?" I asked. I couldn't deny that I was curious to know what had brought the Church Lady to my doorstep this evening.

She lifted her chin. "May I come in, please?"

"Afraid people will see you slumming with me?" I asked, feeling inexplicably hurt by that thought.

"I'd like to have some privacy which, as you know, is darn near impossible in this town."

I opened the door, and she strode in like she owned the place. She looked around, taking in my neat but dated house, then turned to face me.

"Unless I'm misreading the situation, I believe we have a mutual attraction."

I nodded, wondering where this was going.

"As a woman, I have...needs. Needs that, if I'm being honest, have not been met until recently. With you. Given that we are both single as of now, I believe you and I might be able to spend some time together and satisfy those needs."

If this was an attempt at seduction, it was the weirdest one I'd ever had. She sounded like she was trying to sell me life insurance or something.

"Are you asking me to fuck you again, Miz Maribel?"

She flinched slightly, then that spine straightened again. "Yes."

When I didn't respond, she continued, "I've never felt the way I felt with you."

Her voice was soft, almost vulnerable, and that was quite the surprise.

"I want to spend some time exploring my...sensual side and you're quite good at...all that. I came prepared."

And then Miz Maribel unfastened her trench coat and dropped it to the floor, revealing a banging body clad only in a red lace bra and matching panties. My jaw dropped and my heart stopped for so long that I thought I might pass out.

A flush rose up her creamy white skin, and I saw her move as if to wrap her arms around herself, but she caught herself. Instead, she lifted her chin, projecting an air of confidence that I suddenly realized was an affectation she used as a shield.

"You're fucking beautiful," I finally said.

She graced me with a radiant smile that I'd never seen before. I found I quite liked Miz Maribel's smile.

I couldn't stop staring at her curvy body. I'd seen her ass when I'd fucked her from behind in the grocery store, but I had no idea those boring and conservative outfits she wore hid all this. I mean sure, when I fantasized about her all these years, she looked just like this, but I had no idea that would be true in real life.

"What do you say to my proposal?" she asked.

"If we do this, I'm in control, Miz Maribel."

Her eyes darkened, telling me she liked the idea even as she said, "I don't want to be tied up and whipped like in that dirty movie everyone liked."

"And yet you liked it just fine when I spanked your fine ass last week."

To her credit, she didn't deny it.

"I won't hurt you, Miz Maribel. But I won't treat you like fine china either. I've already seen that you like things a little rough. You need things rough, and that's fine with me because I have those same needs. Ain't nothing wrong with that."

I crooked my finger, and she walked closer. I walked around behind her, then unclasped her bra, sliding it down her shoulders and tossing it to the side. I ran my fingers down her spine, fingers counting the bumps in her spine until I met the barrier of her panties. When I slid my finger under the fabric and in between her ass cheeks she gasped.

"Did your husband ever take you back here?"

"No, of course not," she gasped, her voice scandalized.

I slid my finger up and down between her cheeks and she shivered.

"Good. I'll be the first. But not this time."

I stepped back around and got my first glimpse of her breasts. They were full and pendulous, tipped by dark pink circles. Her nipples were distended, pointing straight out as if to greet me. I reached down and gave one a pinch. Maribel gasped, then I pinched the other.

"Take off your panties, Miz Maribel."

I pulled my tee shirt over my head, baring my chest, and I confess I flexed a bit as I saw her admiring my pecs. I relieved myself of my lounge pants next, leaving me standing as naked as the day I was born, same as the prim and proper Maribel Andrews. My cock was jutting straight up, swollen and red.

I stalked towards her, my inner beast gratified when she took a step back, and then another, until her back hit the wall. I caged her in, my palms on the wall on either side of her head, my hard cock pressed against the soft swell of her belly.

Lowering my head, I kissed her. Just like the first time I kissed her, back in the meat locker, it was like putting a match to gasoline. Desire flared, and suddenly our hands were everywhere as my tongue dueled with hers.

When we pulled away, both of us were breathing heavily. I captured her wrists in my hands and pulled them over her head, shackling them in one of my hands. Miz Maribel made the most adorable moaning noise in the back of her throat and arched her back, pointing those glorious breasts in my direction.

I ran my lips down her jaw, then to her neck, where I nibbled along the swell of her shoulder before biting down hard at the junction of her neck and shoulder. She pulled against my grasp as I sucked the skin, not stopping until I'd left her an impressive hickey. I wasn't sure if Maribel thought this was a one-time thing, but if it was, I was going to make sure she had something to remember me by.

"Leave them there," I growled as I released her hands and dropped to my knees. I tapped her ankles, a silent order to spread her legs, and realized she was still wearing her old lady pumps.

I stared at Maribel's pussy for a long moment, noting the moisture already pooled there, before I leaned in and gave her a long lick. Her hips bucked, but she kept her hands up, so I rewarded her with several more.

"Please," she whispered. I wasn't even sure if she knew she'd said it.

Gripping her hips tightly, I began tapping my tongue against the bundle of nerves at her apex. When she was good and squirmy, I sucked her swollen bud into my mouth and bit down slightly. It was enough to set her off like a rocket.

"Oh my Lord! Hank!" Her voice was high and almost surprised as she fluttered against me, my hands on her hips the only thing keeping her standing.

She was still shaking when I rose to my feet again, trailing my hands up her body. She giggled.

"Are you ticklish, Miz Maribel?"

"A little."

I teased her with my fingertips, and she shivered.

"One day you and me are going to have some fun with rope and a feather."

Today was not that day. I wanted her too bad to hold back. Maribel had always been a regular in my spank bank, but since our two encounters, I'd damn near worn the skin off my hand thinking about her. And now that I'd seen what she was hiding under those hideous Church Lady clothes...

Wanting to punish her for distracting me, I wrapped my hand around her throat and pressed just enough to slightly restrict her air. Enough to remind her who was in control. I could feel her pulse fluttering against my finger. I lowered my other hand to cup her pussy and gave that a nice firm squeeze too.

"If we're going to do this, this pussy belongs to me. Only me."

Her eyes widened but she didn't respond, so I squeezed both hands a little more. "Do you understand?"

"Yes," she gasped, then she took a deep breath as I released her.

"Get on your hands and knees," I ordered.

"What?"

I cocked my head, making my face stern. "You heard me."

She must've seen that my expression was serious because she dropped right down to all fours on the floor next to me. I took several long steps across the room.

"Come on."

I wanted to see if she would crawl to me. I needed her to crawl to me. And maybe I believed in God after all, because sure as I was standing here, Miz Maribel crawled over to me.

When she reached me, I petted her head like she was a dog. "Good girl."

I circled her a couple of times, then dropped to my knees behind her.

Thwack!

I couldn't resist smacking that sweet ass. Not when I knew she liked it so much.

Thwack!

Thwack!

Thwack!

I gave her three more good slaps, one on the first side and two on the other side, just to make them even, then admired the tiny stain of pink that raised up on her skin.

"Someday soon I'm going to put you over my knee and use a paddle on you, Miz Maribel."

She made a groaning noise that made me resolve to find that black leather paddle I'd purchased for previous play partners. I didn't always need it to get off or anything, but I did enjoy giving a good paddling on occasion if the woman was amenable. I loved it when a woman gave me the gift of her submission, and I loved watching the moment that the pain turned into pleasure. My Maribel was going to love that, I could tell already.

I tapped her back. "Ass up, head down."

She immediately lowered her upper body to the carpet, head turning to one side. Yeah, Maribel definitely had a submissive side to her.

"Tell me you want my cock."

"Please!"

When I didn't move she added, "Please, I want you so bad!"

It was music to my ears. I gripped her hips hard enough to leave a bruise, then shoved my cock in deep and fast, not giving her any warning. She cried out against the intrusion, her muscles squeezing me so tight I thought she might break my dick right off.

"Relax!" I gave her a sharp slap on the ass.

Her breath whooshed out and she relaxed around me enough so I could start railing her in earnest. I set a hard and brutal pace, my hips connecting with her ass as I slammed into her over and over again. Maribel rocked back against me, shamelessly taking all that she could.

She tightened around me as another orgasm hit her, and I was right behind her, my hips jerking as I started releasing my cum inside her. I'd never had a breeding kink, but right now I wanted nothing more than to put a baby in her belly.

Surprised at that thought, I forced myself to pull out and instead painted the rest of my cum over her ass cheeks. I quite liked how that looked, ropes of white against the pink areas where I'd spanked her good.

Maribel collapsed down on her belly as soon as I pulled out, her face looking almost shell-shocked. I flopped on the floor next to her, laying on my back and turning my face to meet her eyes.

"Are you going to sleep over then Miz Maribel?" I asked.

She nodded, and for the first time since I'd met her, Maribel Andrews looked vulnerable. "If it's okay with you."

"I think that'll be just fine," I responded. "I got me a new pair of nipple clamps I've been saving for someone special."

Hank

"I'm going to spank the pious right out of you!"

Maribel laughed sweetly as I greeted her at the door, the black leather paddle hanging loose in my hand. As usual, she was dressed like some old dowager, today in a boxy black dress that fell halfway down her calves and had a collar that buttoned right up to her throat.

Of course, no one but the two of us knew that the high collar was hiding one hell of a hickey. Maribel had been out of town for work the last two days, and I hadn't been able to resist sending her off with a reminder of who she belonged to.

I don't know which of us was more surprised, but Miz Maribel Andrews and I had come to a mutually beneficial arrangement, something the younger people would call "hooking up". The two of us couldn't be more different, and yet we shared an intense sexual attraction.

Our arrangement was great, except for one tiny snag: after months of sneaking around together, it was starting to feel like more. "Hooking up" became more like "friends with benefits" as Maribel and I got to know each other. Maybe more.

Neither of us would have ever dreamed that Miz Maribel and I had quite a bit in common, but somehow we did.

It was Sunday evening, and I'd gotten home from work about an hour ago. I'd taken a quick shower and whipped us up some dinner as I waited for Maribel to arrive.

"I made us some chicken. Potatoes too."

Maribel's eyes widened in surprise. I wasn't sure whether it was because I could cook, or because I'd made her a meal. I'd never done that before and suddenly I was feeling a bit vulnerable about it.

I pulled her into my house and pressed her against the closed front door, kissing her deeply. When I pulled away, we were both breathing heavy, and I could see her nipples poking right through that ugly dress. She had fabulous nipples.

"Well, you always know how to greet a girl," she said coyly.

I almost asked if she'd missed me, but I held back. We'd agreed to friends with benefits, we'd agreed that I would teach her how to enjoy the kinky shit that she craved, but we'd never agreed to catch feelings.

I threaded her fingers through mine and led her to the kitchen so I could check on the chicken. Seeing it was done, I turned off the heat beneath the pan. I had something I wanted to do first.

"Take off your clothes," I said, my voice turning deep and serious as I pulled out one of the sturdy kitchen chairs. "Get over my lap."

Maribel's eyes widened with excitement. She loved our power and control games just as much as I did. And if that wasn't the damnedest thing.

For years I'd mocked Maribel Andrews — or the Church Lady as I liked to call her — from afar. God knows she was easy to mock, always walking around with a stick up her rear, passing judgment on people from her little church group. Even back when she was in her twenties she'd dressed conservatively, like the wife of some elderly Senator.

Little did I know that beneath those ugly clothes lay racy underwear — purple lace today. And little did I know that beneath her stern exterior there was a funny and caring woman who was also just as kinky as I was.

Maribel laid her now naked body across my lap, bracing her hands on the kitchen floor and I stared down at her, taking a moment to enjoy the sight of her curvy body and unmarked skin.

Thwack!

I brought the leather paddle down on Maribel's incredible ass. The round globe shook from the impact, and within seconds a flush of pink replaced her milky white skin. And in the center, the design of a heart, from the cut-out on the paddle.

Thwack!

Thwack!

I shifted to the other side, brightening up her second butt cheek.

Thwack!

Thwack!

"Ahh!" Maribel's cry was half pain, half pleasure. It was music to my ears.

I knew the balance would switch to mostly pleasure with a few more good spanks. One thing about my Maribel — she craved letting go of her rigid control. She'd spent her entire life with a judgmental and controlling mother who married her off young to a worthless excuse for a man, one who had indiscriminately cheated on her. She'd spent her life keeping an iron-clad control of her own needs and feelings, but now that she was divorced, she was breaking out of her shell and becoming her own woman.

Her submission was a gift I did not take lightly. And after a month of doing whatever we were doing here, I'd learned how to play her body to maximize her pleasure. And giving her pleasure gave *me* pleasure.

Thwack!

She raised her hips to meet the pain, craving it. The sound of the leather cracking across her ass was loud in the quiet room.

Thwack!

Thwack!

Her ass was red as a fire engine now, so I gave her just two more smacks before I dropped the paddle. Using the lightest touch, I soothed her skin while she cooed beneath me like a baby bird.

"How was that?" I asked as I helped her move to standing. She wobbled a bit, as if her legs were weak, and I grabbed her waist to steady her.

"Incredible." Her voice was as soft as her face. "Just what I needed."

She dropped to her knees between my legs, unzipping my jeans. Her eyes widened as she realized that I'd forgone my boxers, but she didn't comment. Instead, she took me in hand, her thumb catching the beads of pre-cum at the tip of my cock and spreading it along the mushroom head.

She lowered her head, but I stopped her long enough to pull the pins out of her long blonde hair. Maribel tightly controlled her hair, always wearing it in a severe bun, and I loved the fact that I was the only one who got to see her with her hair streaming over her shoulders in a wild disarray.

When her hair was free, Maribel wrapped her lips around my straining cock and slowly moved up and down a few times. It didn't take long before my own need for control took over, and I gripped her head in my hands and began to roughly fuck her mouth.

Maribel gripped my knees as I pushed her face up and down, tapping against the back of her throat with every thrust. Saliva pooled in her mouth and ran down the sides of her chin, and when I took my cock out, her lips were red and swollen.

"I wonder what those old biddies in your church would say if they could see you now," I mused.

Those stern matrons would swallow their damn crosses if they knew that their beloved member let me fuck her in a meat locker. They'd call out for Jesus himself if they knew that their precious Maribel had once given me a blow job on the side of the road. And if they knew how much she loved it when I spanked her ass red and then fucked her from behind like some kind of animal, well, that might just kill them.

Sooner or later the word would get out that Maribel and I had been spending time together and the judgment would fall down on both of us. Not that I gave a good goddamn about other people's opinions. But I knew Maribel worried about it.

Honestly, I was amazed we'd been able to keep it a secret this long. Our small town traded gossip like it was currency. We never went out in public, a fact that was starting to bother me if I was honest, but it was a miracle no one had seen us coming and going from each other's houses at all hours.

For right now, I was relishing our privacy.

I reached out and palmed Maribel's tits, squeezing them the way those old church ladies squeezed melons at my family's grocery store. She leaned into my touch as I turned my attention to her nipples, pulling and squeezing them.

When I was finished with her, those cute pink nipples were poking out nicely. I reached into my pocket and took out a pair of nipple clamps. My Maribel both loved them and hated them.

She gasped as I clipped one clamp to her left nipple, then affixed the other one to the right side. They were held together by a thin chain, and when I pulled on it, Maribel moaned at the increased pressure.

I patted my lap. "Hop on up here and ride me, Miz Maribel."

She rose to her feet, then straddled my lap, one knee coming to each side of my chair. Gripping her hips, I shifted her to line us up, then slammed her down onto my aching cock. We both groaned as our hips met, her pussy squeezing me like a goddamned vise.

I lifted her slowly up, then dropped her back down, again and again. I watched as each drop made her breasts bob up and down, pulling on the nipple clamps until her nipples looked red and angry.

Tightening my fingers on her hips until she cried out, I started slamming her up and down even harder, fucking myself with her, totally in control. She loved it though. Her eyes were bright, her mouth open, her fingers digging into my shoulders for balance as she made tiny sounds of pleasure.

"Oh my God, Hank," she gasped. "That feels so good."

My Maribel didn't talk a lot during sex, but I knew that when she got more vocal she was getting close to a good, solid orgasm.

"Do you like me using you like a fuck toy, Miz Maribel?"

"You know I do."

"Tell me that you're my little slut," I demanded. I knew she liked a little humiliation talk as much as I did. "Tell me how much you want my cum."

"I'm your slut. Please Hank, please give me your cum."

The next time I dropped her to my lap I yanked off the nipple clamps, and she screamed as the blood returned to her nipples in a blaze of fiery pain. Not ten seconds later she started moaning, bucking against me as another hard orgasm rolled through her body. Her body spasmed so hard she damn near fell off of me.

"Ahhh!"

Her pussy squeezed me tight, and I continued fucking her roughly until I felt my own release tingle at the base of my spine. I pulled out just as my dick damn near exploded, shooting my jizz all over her stomach, pussy, and thighs.

When I was done I looked down, happy with my handiwork.

Leaning forward, I gave her a long kiss. I could kiss this woman forever. Maybe I would.

As I leaned back, she gave me a small smile. "I should get cleaned up."

"Oh no you don't Miz Maribel, I want you to put that ugly dress back on and have dinner with me. I like knowing that you have the evidence of your sinner side underneath that saintly garment."

She rolled her eyes at my ridiculous words but complied, moseying over to pick up her dress and pull it over her head. She gathered her underwear and tossed it toward the purse she'd dropped by the front door. I guess I wasn't the only one going commando over dinner.

I grabbed a dish towel and cleaned up before zipping myself back in and heading back towards the stove where I'd left dinner warming.

"You like fried chicken don'tcha, Miz Maribel?" I asked her.

"I sure do. I love it."

"Perfect. Why don't you have a seat at the table while I serve you up a plate then."

I smiled over the pan of chicken as I heard the yelp when her aggrieved backside made contact with the hard chair.

"Something the matter?" I asked with a laugh.

"No sir, everything's perfect."

That might have been the truest thing the Church Lady had ever said.

Maribel

"I think you're ready to lose your virginity."

I looked across the table at my secret boyfriend, Hank Parsons. No one who knew either of us would put us together. Hank was younger, rougher, rode a motorcycle – and worst of all for the people I'd been surrounded with since I was a baby in my Mama's arms – he never went to church.

It had been a good four months since the day we'd gotten into an argument over a pork loin, and he'd pounded into me from behind in a meat locker. I think we'd both thought it was a fluke, but then somehow I'd found myself giving him a blowjob on the side of the road and I'd realized two things: I'd gone my entire life without having good sex, and I kind of liked Hank Parsons.

I'd proposed a friends with benefits arrangement, which had somehow turned into us secretly dating. In the months we'd been together we'd explored all my fantasies: spanking, being tied up, choking, and rough fucking in every position imaginable.

As Hank placed a rectangular box on the table I knew we were about to explore one of his fantasies: taking my anal cherry.

As a good Christian woman, I'd never once even considered letting anyone touch me back there. Then again, I'd spent my entire life married to a man who thought having sex in the spooning position was adventurous. Somehow I had a feeling that my ex-husband had been a little more creative with the long line of sluts he'd fucked while were married. But that was just a guess.

Hank had been hinting about anal for quite some time now, and I had to admit that I was curious.

I pushed my empty dinner plate to the side and lifted the lid off the box. Inside were two blue silicone butt plugs, one smaller, one larger. I examined them carefully. They looked like little conifer trees or maybe some weird baby pacifiers. Even the smaller one looked like it was a little too big to go into its intended spot.

Looking up, I saw Hank watching me carefully, waiting for my response.

"Okay, I'm game."

There was a quick flash of relief before he schooled his face into the stern expression he liked to affect when he was playing Dom.

Since my divorce ten months ago, I'd made it a point to be my own woman. To be strong and independent. I'd promised myself I'd never submit to anyone else's will again. And I intended to stick to that resolution. Except in bed. There was one person in the world I was willing to trust with my submission, and that was Hank.

"Let's get you ready."

Hank grabbed my hand and led me into the bedroom. "Take off your clothes."

I didn't hesitate to comply, removing my clothes and setting them on a chair while he rummaged around in a drawer. When he turned, he was holding a container of lube.

"Lean over the bed."

I settled my stomach on the bed, resting my head on my folded arms, my ass sticking out.

Thwack!

His hand came down in a hard slap, quickly followed by another.

Thwack!

My boyfriend knew the best way to relax me. That's right, somewhere along the way my hook-up became my boyfriend. Not that anyone else knew about it yet.

After a few more hard spanks, my butt cheeks were stinging. I gasped as I felt the coolness of the lube hit my ass crack. Hank slipped one thick finger between my cheeks, spreading the lube as I shivered in anticipation.

He poured out more lube, squirting directly towards the puckered rosebud that had never been breached with anything more than the tip of Hank's playful finger from time to time. He pressed his finger in, slick with lube, and pushed it in and out a few times, spreading the lube. After repeating the process a second time, I heard him squeeze out more lube, presumably on the butt plug this time.

"You know Miz Maribel, I was planning to start with the smaller one but it's barely more than a finger or two. I think you can take more."

I stiffened as I felt the hardness of the silicone against my asshole.

Thwack!

"Relax!"

The tip breached my opening, and I realized it already felt bigger than I expected. How the hell was I going to take Hank's monster cock?

Thwack!

Hank slid it in a bit more before my butt cheek had stopped jiggling from his hard smack.

"Push out a bit, it'll go in easier if you can relax."

Thwack!

Another smack and the butt plug breached the tight ring of muscles, seating inside me. It felt...weird. Not bad, not good, just weird. And naughty as hell. Hank slid the plug in and out a few times, rotating it, and as I became more comfortable, it felt better and better.

"Let's get you used to this first, in the meantime, I've got a treat for you for taking your plug like a good girl."

Hank hopped up on the bed, still fully clothed, and settled himself on the pillows.

"Hop on up here Miz Maribel," he said, gesturing at his face. "Lemme have some dessert."

I stood up, wiggling a bit at the fullness in my backside, then crawled up Hank's body and arranged my knees on both sides of his shoulders. Strong hands came to my hips, pulling me down, and I felt the roughness of his thick tongue sliding between my folds.

"You're dripping wet you naughty girl, I think you like having me breach that sweet ass of yours."

I couldn't deny that the longer the plug was in there, the more excited I got. It was deliciously dirty. Sinful. And I'd learned to love being sinful.

Hank focused his attention on my clit, tapping and circling the little bundle of nerves, holding me close until I finally broke apart. I gripped the headboard, damn near smothering him as I desperately ground my pussy against his face and cried out his name.

"Hank!"

I pushed back, dropping onto his chest, then yelping as the movement pressed against the butt plug. I rolled over to my side instead, resting my head on Hank's face as I caught my breath. My eyes traveled down, noticing the telltale bulge of his erection pressing against his jeans.

"That looks painful," I teased, reaching down to rub him.

"Don't tease me, little girl," he growled.

I couldn't help but laugh. In a flash, Hank had me flat on my back, trapped under his weight, his tongue in my mouth as he gave me a long, claiming kiss. As he pulled back, I bit my tongue to keep from telling him that I loved him. I'd been hurt before and as much as I trusted Hank, I wasn't going to be the first one to put myself out there.

Hank rolled his hips against my core, fucking me through his clothes. I reached up and cupped his face between my palms.

"I'm ready."

Never in a million years would I have thought this could happen, but right now I wanted nothing more than to feel Hank's cock in my ass.

He jumped off the bed and shucked his clothes while I admired his fit body. The man was built like a linebacker, a position he'd played in high school. When he was a kid he thought he'd head for the NFL when he grew up, but he wasn't good enough to do more than play some ball in college. I knew it was probably his biggest disappointment in life.

Instead, he'd gotten a degree in business and come back to the small town where he'd grown up, taking over his Daddy's grocery store.

"Get back where you were," Hank ordered, his voice gruff. "Feet on the floor, ass up."

I moved into position, then Hank lifted me up enough to shove a sturdy pillow beneath my belly, angling my hips up more. His hands squeezed my butt cheeks a few times, then he slid his hand between them and slowly removed the plug. It came out a bit easier than it went in.

"I'm not going to lie Miz Maribel, this is gonna hurt at first, but I know you like pain."

God help me, he was right.

I looked over my shoulder to see him applying a thick rope of lube over his cock, rubbing it in with his hand to make sure he was slick all around. He stepped closer, one big hand coming to each butt cheek, spreading me wide. I turned my head, pressing my face into the comforter.

The tip of his cock pressed against me, circling around my opening a couple of times before pressing against me, demanding entrance. Hank squeezed me with his hands, hard enough to bruise.

"Focus on the pain, relax into the pain."

My Hank wasn't a sweet talker, but he knew exactly what to say. I turned all my attention to the burning as he slid in slowly, stopping as he reached the ring of my sphincter, then punching through.

"FUUCK!"

It was literally the first time I'd said that word out loud in my nearly forty years on this Earth, but damned if it didn't feel like Hank was fixing to split me right in half. The hot burning pain was as intense as anything I'd felt before.

He retreated back slowly, still staying inside me, then slid back in deeper. Over and over, he slid back, then moved forward until finally, finally his huge balls pressed against my pussy, telling me he was fully seated.

We both stilled for a long moment, then he began moving, slowly at first, gradually picking up speed. And damned if it didn't feel way better than I was expecting. Hank was stimulating something in there that was making me tingle in excitement.

As so often happened when Hank and I explored our fantasies, what started as pain soon turned to incredible pleasure.

"I thought your pussy was tight," Hank grunted, "but this, this is fucking incredible."

He moved one hand to the back of my neck, holding me down, asserting his dominance in a way that only ramped up my excitement. A second hand slid around my hips, finding my clit.

In an instant, it was all too much. Hank's weight pressing me into the bed. His fingers roughly circling my swollen clit, and that huge cock pounding into my ass, stretching me wider than I ever thought was possible.

"Hank!"

The orgasm shocked me with its intensity. I tried to escape from the overwhelming sensations, but I was helpless to do anything but let the waves of intense pleasure roll through me until I was sobbing out my release.

I was still shaking with aftershocks when Hank's hands returned to my hips, his movements becoming erratic as he came with a shout.

"Maribel. I fucking love you!"

I felt the warmth of his cum filling my back channel as he thrust inside me a few more times, then collapsed over my back. He dotted kisses on the back of my neck and along my shoulder before pushing himself back up. He slowly pulled out and I felt surprisingly empty as I lay there, completely exhausted.

"Come on up here, baby," Hank said, gently maneuvering me up to the bed and into his arms.

I cuddled into his side, throwing my arm across his stomach, and resting my head on his chest. One large hand moved slowly up and down my back and over the curve of my ass, soothing me.

"How was it?" he finally asked. "Did I hurt you?"

I looked up to meet his eyes and gave him a smile. "Only in the best way."

"I meant what I said before. I do love you Miz Maribel."

I cuddled back down against him, feeling happier than anyone had a right to be. "I love you too."

Epilogue - Maribel

Some men propose with flowers. Some with a grand gesture. My boyfriend? He proposed by tying me to the bed and dropping a ring box on my belly button.

It all started on Christmas Eve.

Nearly a year had gone by since Hank and I first realized our attraction and had what we both thought was going to be a mindless fuck in his grocery store. But then he helped me fix my car — and I'd given him a nice blow job to thank him — and I found I couldn't get him out of my mind. I proposed a casual fuck buddies kind of thing, but eventually, we'd somehow developed feelings for each other, and well, here we were.

It hadn't been an easy year and a half for me. Over eighteen months I'd gotten divorced, started dating someone new for the first time in twenty years, put up with a bunch of crap from my so-called friends at church about my "inappropriate choice of boyfriends", and come to some difficult realizations about my life spent listening to what everyone else told me I should do.

Now Hank was the only one who told me what to do, and that was strictly in bed.

Some good things had come out of this period too. I'd started speaking my mind, thinking for myself, and exploring all of my secret desires that I'd told myself were sinful. And maybe they were, but I couldn't bring myself to care, not when it felt so good.

At first, everything with me and Hank had been rough and kinky, but as we'd gotten closer, we came to enjoy lovemaking as much as we enjoyed sex. I'd learned the difference, and maybe Hank had too.

We were an odd couple, but we worked. I knew for a fact I was the first woman he'd dated for more than a few months. And he was the first man to make me orgasm, the first man to tie me up, and the first man to show me what all the fuss was about anal.

Tonight was Christmas Eve, and Hank had kept the store open late for last-minute holiday food shopping. Hank's family owned Parson's Grocery Store, the only supermarket in our tiny town, and he took his responsibility to his community quite seriously.

I greeted Hank wearing nothing but a "Kiss Me I'm Santa's Helper" apron and a smile.

"Welcome home," I said, going up on tiptoes and giving him a kiss.

His firm lips came down on mine, his tongue shoving between my teeth to sweep my mouth like an invading conqueror. I was breathless when we pulled apart. Kissing Hank always did that to me.

"I love it when you wear your hair down," he whispered, one hand stroking my blonde locks.

Normally I wore my hair tightly restrained but when I was with Hank I let my hair down both literally and figuratively.

"Wait a minute, what are you wearing, you naughty girl?"

I was surprised that it took so long for him to notice that I was only wearing an apron. I gave him an impish grin and spun around, giving him an eyeful of my bare backside. I might be eight years older than him, but I kept myself in good shape thanks to regular sessions with a personal trainer at the gym. And according to Hank, my ass was my best feature.

"I ought to spank you for walking around like that," he growled, his eyes sparkling.

"I was hoping you would."

Another thing I'd learned over the last year: nothing calmed my mind like a good hard spanking from my boyfriend.

"Get the paddle."

I shivered at the intent in his gaze. I headed over to the kitchen drawer where I'd stashed the paddle for exactly this moment. It was made out of soft black leather, with a heart insert cut out near the top.

"Get over the arm of the couch," Hank ordered, his voice deep and low.

I walked slowly towards the living room, adding a little shake to my hips to tease him. Hank gave me a tap on the ass with his palm as I walked by, causing me to jump.

I lowered myself over the arm of the couch, bracing my hands on the cushion and putting my ass on full display. The apron fell forward, causing my heavy breasts to hang between my arms.

Thwack!

The first smack with the paddle made my skin sting. I could feel my flesh jiggling a bit from the impact. I sighed happily.

Thwack!

Thwack!

Hank began a steady rhythm, moving the black leather paddle from one side to the other, covering every inch of my ass with precision. My skin heated and I moaned softly as the hamster wheel in my head went still, calming my thoughts.

Thwack!

Thwack!

I was raised to be a pious church-going lady who dressed and acted respectably at all times. My mama taught me that women shouldn't get pleasure from sex, that it was all about procreation and pleasing our husbands so they wouldn't leave.

I'd done everything my husband ever asked, but that still hadn't been enough for him. I'd saved myself for marriage and stayed faithful to him despite his many, many shortcomings, but he hadn't given me the same courtesy.

It was ironic that a man who couldn't find the clitoris if his life depended on it was such a popular lover before he'd been run out of town in disgrace.

Thwack!

Thwack!

My rear end felt like it was on fire, but with every smack of the paddle, pain and pleasure melded into something delicious. I raised my hips, eager to meet the paddle on every downward stroke.

I yelped as Hank varied his routine, striking me on the back of the thighs, right where they connected to my butt. Damn, that was a tender spot. He gave me just a couple of smacks there, then dropped the paddle. It hit the carpet with a soft thud, then Hank eased his fingers over my aggrieved skin, soothing me a bit.

Moving his hands up my shoulders, Hank pulled me up to standing, spun me around, and backed me to the wall. He unzipped his pants just enough to free that enormous cock of his, then lifted me up against the wall and slammed into my pussy so hard that I thought for sure the drywall would crack behind me.

"Do you...like...dressing slutty?" He asked between thrusts.

His breath was labored enough that I knew he wouldn't last long.

"Only for you."

I hooked my feet behind his waist and gripped his shoulders for balance, meeting him stroke for stroke. Hank boosted me up higher, coming at me from another angle, and lowered his mouth to my shoulder, giving me a nice love bite. Lord, the man loved to bite. I was forever covered in little marks from his teeth. As he sucked my skin between his lips and clamped his teeth on me, an orgasm rolled through my body like a tsunami.

"Hank!"

I shuddered against him, trapped between his body and the wall, unable to do anything but succumb to the intense pleasure. When it was over, I'd left marks on his shoulders from my fingernails.

"Maribel!"

Hank stiffened, then thrust in deep, his warm cum releasing in a long spurt. He pulled back with a growl, then slammed back in deeper, more of his seed coming to coat the walls of my womb. I had an IUD that

I used to control erratic periods, and I suddenly wondered if I got it removed if I could get pregnant despite being nearly forty.

I'd never once considered having a child before. I knew my ex-husband thought I was infertile, probably because I'd kept my IUD a secret from him. I guess part of me always knew that the lying, cheating scumbag would leave me high and dry someday.

Hank sagged against me, his head on my shoulder, his breathing ragged. My feet slid back to the floor as he pulled away, careful to keep me from dropping. Our eyes met and held, and I saw love and lust there in equal measure.

I felt the same way.

He stepped forward, grabbing my waist and flipping me up and over his shoulder like a sack of potatoes. I grabbed onto his waistband for balance as he carried me into his bedroom.

Our bedroom now. I'd moved in with him a few months ago. We were "living in sin" now, much to the horror of my pastor and several women I used to call friends.

I hadn't realized how backward and puritanical some members of our town were until I'd incurred their wrath by living my own life, making my own decisions, and daring to be happy for the first time in my life. Hank made me happy in a way no one else had ever done before.

We were about three feet away from the bed when Hank gave me a toss. I laughed as I bounced on the mattress.

"There you go again, manhandling me."

He did that thing that guys do where he reached over his head to pull off his "Parson's Grocery" tee shirt, then got to work removing his unzipped jeans and boxers. He was wearing a pair of boxers I'd given him a few months ago that had big pink lips on them. I told him I wanted him to think about my mouth on his cock every time he wore them.

That was another thing about me that was different now. I'd gone almost forty years without using words like "cock" or "pussy" or — God forbid — "fuck", but now I felt a bit more comfortable expressing myself with profanity.

Across town, my poor dead mama was rolling in her grave at the thought.

Hank removed the apron I was wearing and then pulled my hands overhead, using the apron strings to tie me securely to the slats of the headboard. Once he'd gotten me tied good and tight, he reached into the bottom drawer of the bedside table and pulled out the Magic Wand.

The monster vibrator started buzzing loudly. There was no way you could hide and use that thing, it was like the industrial version of a vibrator. It looked like some kind of weird massager, nothing like our other toys that were more anatomically correct.

With an evil smile, Hank sat himself on the bed next to me and slid the Magic Wand through my dripping folds.

"Ahh!"

The vibrations felt rough on my already tender skin.

"You can take it."

He was right, I could. Hank slid the vibrator back and forth a few more times, then settled the bulbous head of the Magic Wand right over my clit. I jerked as the intense vibrations moved over the swollen bundle of nerves.

Instinctively I tried to move away, but Hank clamped his other hand down on my hip, holding me still. I struggled against his hold but between the strength of his grip and my hands firmly tied above me, all I could do was kick my legs against the sensation.

Hank circled around my clit, then homed right back in, pressing down until my clit was trapped between my pubic bone and the Magic Wand. Less than a minute later I came so damn hard that for the first time in my entire life I squirted as I succumbed to my orgasm.

I screeched loud enough to shatter glass as wave after wave of intense pleasure rolled through my body, leaving me a boneless and incoherent mess.

I was scarcely aware of Hank turning off the vibrator and walking away from the bed. He walked over to the dresser and rummaged around in a drawer while I watched him curiously.

"Close your eyes."

I screwed my eyes shut and felt the sensation of something light landing on my stomach.

"Open your eyes."

I automatically glanced down, seeing saw a small, blue velvet box sitting right on top of my belly button.

"What's that?"

Hank looked a little nervous for the first time in our acquaintance.

"Marry me."

"Huh?"

Honestly, if I hadn't already been laying down, he could have knocked me over with one of those feathers he liked to torture me with when I was tied up like this.

"Marry me," he said again.

"You're asking me to marry you while I'm tied to the bed buck naked?" I screeched in horror.

"Yep."

I couldn't help but laugh. "You don't have a romantic bone in your body, do you Hank Parsons?"

"We don't need romantic baby, we got something real here."

I rolled my eyes. "Let me see the ring."

He opened the box and I saw the glint of light from the tiny diamond surrounded by two small rubies. A warm glow of happiness filled my chest. He might not be romantic, but Hank knew me well enough to pick out the perfect ring.

"It's beautiful."

He looked relieved. My Hank was one of those cinnamon roll guys – he seemed tough and hard on the outside, but he had a squishy center.

"How about you untie me so I can try it on?"

***

If you liked this book, please consider leaving a review or rating on my author page to let me know.

Don't forget to join my newsletter and receive a copy of my book "Hotwife Happy Hour" for free. My newsletter subscribers are the first to hear about all of my new releases and sales. Visit my mailing list sign-up[1] at bit.ly/rebabooks to get your free book today.

Be sure to keep reading for a free preview of Reba Bale's MFM menage romance "Summer in Paradise," available now.

---

1.   *https://storyoriginapp.com/giveaways/495308f4-2d9f-11ed-bfd5-c7ccde0cb7e8*

Special Preview

Summer in Paradise
A MFM Romance
By Reba Bale

"Mmm. Smell that fresh ocean air!"

I turned to my best friend Mike with a smile. "This is going to be epic."

A voluptuous woman in a very small bikini top and a floral sarong walked by with a tray of glasses. "Daquiri?"

"Thanks, sweetheart," I said, taking two glasses and handing one to Mike. I took a big sip of the frosty drink. "I could get used to this."

The people in front of us walked away and the desk clerk beckoned us forward with a warm smile. "Welcome to Temptation in Paradise, are you checking in?"

"Hello. Yes, I have a reservation under Dylan Cramer."

The woman tapped away at the computer. "We're glad to have you with us this week Mr. Cramer. I've got you in the Ocean Breeze Cabana. Here are your keys." She slid two key cards across the desk, each attached to a strap. "You can loop these on your belt or wear them around your wrist. They're totally waterproof."

"Great, thanks."

She took out two yellow strips.

"These are your wristbands. They identify you as guests of the resort and must be worn at all times while you're here." She gestured towards my hand. "If you'll give me your wrist..."

Once she had affixed wristbands on Mike and me, she took out a map and placed it on the counter.

"Here we are," she started, drawing a circle around the picture of a building marked as reception. "Your cabana is over here, you head right when you exit this building, and follow the path around. Each cabana has a different name which is on a sign outside."

Mike and I nodded, following the movement of the pen as she drew a line across the map from where we were to where we are going, then pointed out several other parts of the property.

"We have four dining rooms here, here, here, and here," she continued, making a little X by each one. "The pool is here, the recreation areas are here, the spa is here, and the nightclub is here. The dungeon is in the same building."

"I'm sorry, did you say dungeon?" Mike asked.

She nodded, her expression coy. "For our guests who are into BDSM or want to try a scene. It's fully equipped with everything you need."

My face must have indicated my confusion because she added, "We have staff who can teach you how to safely explore BDSM if you're new to the lifestyle."

"Wow, OK."

"Clothing is optional anywhere in the resort except for the dining areas. The health department requires people to have clothing and shoes in those spaces."

I was starting to realize that this place was not exactly what we thought it was.

Her sweet tone suddenly turned stern. "It goes without saying, but there is absolutely no photographs or filming allowed. You will be immediately excluded from the resort if you violate the privacy of another guest, and we will press charges with local authorities."

She handed us another piece of paper, back to being friendly. "Here is a list of all of our activities for the week. Every day has a different fun theme. We're having a partner swap party tonight on the back deck if you two want to swing with another couple."

I felt a flush rise to my face. "We're not uh, together. Not that there's anything wrong with that, but we're just friends."

The woman looked amused. "Well as we say here at Temptation in Paradise, anything goes as long as it's consensual. That's why we are the premiere adult resort in the Bahamas. You guys have fun, and please pop over to the concierge desk or give us a call if you need any help with anything. Enjoy your week with us."

"Thank you."

I glanced at my best friend as we walked outside, but he wasn't looking at me. His wide eyes were fixed on something to his right. I glanced over and nearly stumbled over my own feet as I saw a woman bent over a picnic table, a man pumping into her from behind. They were both completely naked. The woman smiled over at us, clearly enjoying herself and unfazed at being watched. I couldn't help the flush that rose up my face at the sight. I had never seen someone having sex outside of a porno, besides myself of course.

"Um, Mike, I don't think this place is exactly what we thought it was," I said as we continued walking in the direction of our cabana.

Mike and I were best friends. We'd both started at the same company after graduation from business school. We'd hit it off at new employee orientation, and due to the high price of housing in our area, we soon became roommates. We had been working long enough now that we could probably afford our own places, but we both loved the two bedroom apartment we'd rented not that far from our office. We had the top floor in a converted Victorian and great neighbors, so we were pretty comfortable right where we were.

A couple of months ago our company had announced a quarterly sales competition, with the winner receiving an all-expenses paid trip for two to a tropical resort. I'd won, but Mike came in second, so it was a no-brainer to invite him as my plus-one, especially since the boss had set us up in a two-bedroom cabana. He'd told us that this was an adults only resort, which I think we both assumed meant there were no kids allowed, but I was starting to understand that in this context, 'adults only' meant something else entirely. I guess I should have looked at their website before we came.

"I didn't even know there were these type of resorts like this in real life," Mike said as we walked by a game of naked volleyball.

"Me neither. This place looks like something out of a high quality porno."

"I guess there's a good chance we'll get laid on this trip," Mike laughed. "We might as well enjoy it."

For more of the story, check out "Summer in Paradise" by Reba Bale, available for immediate purchase on your favorite retail sites[1] today.

***

Want a free book? Join my newsletter and receive a free copy of my book "Hotwife Happy Hour" for free. I promise I will only email you when there are new releases or special sales, so visit bit.ly/rebabooks and sign up today.

---

1.   https://books2read.com/u/bwKPV0

Other Books by Reba Bale

Check out my other books, available on most major online retailers now. Go to my webpage[1] to learn more.

The Spanking Therapy Series

The Reluctant Bride's First Spanking

The Reluctant Bride Gets Caught

The Billionaire Gets Punished

The Divorce Recovery Series

Spanking Justice: A Middle-Aged Divorcee's First Spanking

A Punishing Workout: Spanked by the Trainer

A Disciplined Budget: Spanked by the Accountant

The Curvy Reporter Gets Punished

Unlikely Doms Series

Alpha in a Sweater Vest

Alpha Plumber

Hotel Spanking

Alpha Student

Alpha Yogi

The Voyeur Romance Series

Naughty Sunbathing

Naughty Dinner Date

Naughty Laundry Date

Naughty Camping

Paying for Tuition

The Babysitter's Ride Home

The Babysitter's First Menage

The Teaching Assistant's Lesson

The Billionaire's Assistant

The Marriage Survival Series

---

1. https://books2read.com/ap/nB2qJv/Reba-Bale

About the Author

Reba Bale loves writing naughty stories where the characters are able to tap into their inner fantasies and experience spanking, bondage, humiliation, or other activities on the non-vanilla side of life. When Reba is not writing she is reading the same naughty stories she likes to write.

You can also follow Reba on Medium[2] for free stories, bonus epilogues and more. You can also hear all about new releases and special sales by joining Reba's newsletter mailing list.[3]

2.　　https://medium.com/@authorrebabale

3.　　https://bit.ly/rebabooks

Don't miss out!

Visit the website below and you can sign up to receive emails whenever Reba Bale publishes a new book. There's no charge and no obligation.

https://books2read.com/r/B-A-IDTM-LDWCC

BOOKS2READ

Connecting independent readers to independent writers.

Did you love *Sinful Desires*? Then you should read *Taken by Surprise*[4] by Reba Bale!

A masked man. A night of passion. An unexpected revelation...

After months of social distancing Christy has pandemic fatigue. She needs to socialize. She needs to talk to someone who is not on Zoom. She needs...to scratch an itch. A year of isolation is a long time to be alone with nothing but her battery-operated boyfriend to keep her company. When her friend suggests they get together in real life and attend an underground masquerade party downtown, Christy decides it's worth the risk.

She shares an incredible night with a total stranger, but when the masks come off and she realizes that she had the hottest night of her

---

4. https://books2read.com/u/3GrE9a

5. https://books2read.com/u/3GrE9a

life with is actually her new boss, will she regret her decision to break quarantine?

"Taken by Surprise" is book one of the "Dancing with Strangers" series. Each book is a steamy standalone erotic romance featuring a curvy woman, an older alpha billionaire, a costume party, and a satisfying happily ever after. This book includes explicit sexual activity between consenting adults. It is intended for mature audiences only.

Also by Reba Bale

Affair Recovery
Share Me: A Cheating Husband's Punishment

Dancing with Strangers
Taken by Surprise

Friends to Lovers
The Divorcee's First Time: A Hot Friends-to-Lovers Lesbian Romance
My BFF's Sister
My Rockstar Assistant
My College Crush
My Fake Girlfriend
My Secret Crush
My Holiday Love
My Valentine's Gift
My Spring Fling

Paying for Tuition

The Billionaire's Assistant
The Babysitter's Ride Home
The Babysitter's First Ménage
The Teaching Assistant's Lesson

Punishing Holidays
Turkey and a Spanking
Shopping and a Spanking

Sharing With Strangers
The Ride of My Life

Spanking Therapy Clinic
The Reluctant Bride's First Spanking
The Reluctant Bride Gets Caught
The Billionaire Gets Punished
The Curvy Reporter Gets Punished

The Divorce Recovery Team
Spanking Justice
A Punishing Workout
A Disciplined Budget

The Marriage Survival Retreat
Finding His Alpha

Watching His Wife
Exploring His Fantasy

The Voyeur Romance Series
Naughty Dinner Date
Naughty Laundry Day
Naughty Camping
Naughty Love Story
Naughty Sunbathing

Toys for Grown-Ups
Ménage a Geek
Financial Punishment

Unlikely Doms
Alpha in a Sweater Vest
Alpha Student
Alpha Yogi

Standalone
Hotel Spanking
Unlikely Doms
Divorce Recovery Team: A Punishment Experiment Collection
Spicing Up My Marriage
It Takes Three
The Christmas Swap

Sinful Desires